CHASE-ING
Clouds

WRITTEN BY

Julie Brown

ILLUSTRATED BY

Kara Lynn Daviau

Archway Publishing books may be ordered through booksellers or by contacting:

Archway Publishing
1663 Liberty Drive
Bloomington, IN 47403
www.archwaypublishing.com
844-669-3957

Interior Image Credit: Kara Lynn Daviau

ISBN: 978-1-6657-4187-3 (sc)
ISBN: 978-1-6657-4188-0 (hc)
ISBN: 978-1-6657-4186-6 (e)

Print information available on the last page.

Archway Publishing rev. date: 04/26/2023

Inspiration behind
CHASE-ING *Clouds*

Every expecting family goes to the hospital with the anticipation of bringing home their beautiful newborn baby. In some unfortunate and devastating circumstances, perception and reality do not match. Such as the case with Chase. When his parents got to the hospital to deliver him, they received the unthinkable news that Chase didn't have a heartbeat, and he would be born an angel. Chase's parents left the hospital with a hole in their hearts, as opposed to the bundle of joy in their arms they had envisioned.

Everyone deserves the opportunity to leave their imprint on this world. Chase's imprint was different than anyone expected, but there were bigger plans for him. Plans that would allow his legacy to inspire from above.

Our hope is that you can find comfort in the pages of this book, knowing that anytime you're missing a loved one, you can look up and find them in the clouds, and know they are always with you.

Whether you are in the thick of grief, or sadness comes and goes, know that you are never alone, just gaze at the sky.

Do you ever look up at the sky, and notice the clouds passing by?

Maybe they start turning into shapes,
like superheroes wearing capes.

You begin to chase them along,
because you believe in them,
and know you aren't wrong.

You start to think, did someone
send them just for me?
Could it really be?

Sometimes our loved ones
have to leave, and we
can't understand why.
But don't worry, just look
up, and you'll find them
in the clouds passing by.

Look up in the sky, what do you see?
Do you see a rainbow of beautiful
colors, of all different shades?
Are we sliding down slides, or marching in parades?

Remember the time we ate that delicious ice cream sundae, with mounds of whipped cream? It had a perfectly red round cherry on top, and we thought to ourselves, "Wow, this must be a dream."

8

When you look up at the sky, do you see gigantic
clouds of pink and blue cotton candy?
Do you get the giggles and squeals, the kind
that make you feel joyful and dandy?

Maybe you see that familiar, happy wagging tail. Although I'm across the rainbow bridge, I'll always be your best pal.

As you glance up high,
do you see waves in
shades of blue?
Watching the back and
forth motion as they
crash into me and you.
We run in and out trying
not to get wet.
We have to be fast,
don't forget!

Can you hear the birds chirping and
feel the sun warming our faces?
Better get going, and tie up our laces.
Let's head to the park where we'll have a catch.
First you throw to me, then me to you,
oh we're such a great match!

Take a look out your window, it's starting to snow!
Some fluffy and big, some so small
they disappear on a twig.
As we watch the snowflakes dance and fall together,
I hope you remember this feeling forever.

"Vroom, Vroom," what's that you say? You're
here to pick me up and drive away?
The top is down, the wind blowing in our
hair, and I can't help but stare.
These are the moments we share when you dream.
I live them with you, right by your side,
for we make the best team.

"Fore!" you say.
As we take our golf clubs
and swing away.
I'm always there cheering,
as I watch you perfect
your swing.
We go from hole to hole
and finish our game.
Always remember, when
you're missing me, just
call out my name.

15

"Mmmm," I can smell your cooking.
The delicious vanilla and sugar, I don't
even need to go looking.
I'm here to help you with your baking.
Your cookies, so yummy, I can't stop myself from taking.
The ones I love the most, I can taste in my dreams.
Some are filled with chocolate, others filled with creams.

It's time for bed,
come snuggle in close, head to head.
I'll read one page, you the next.
I always leave you the last word of the text.

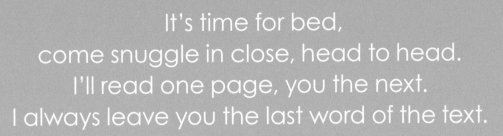

When you turn over to go to sleep,
I hope you feel me there, as you
begin to count sheep.

Whenever you feel that
tug at your heart,
I want you to know, we
are never far apart.
Look up at the sky and the clouds.

See us together, and be happy
for the time we were allowed.
And even though we
wished it was longer,
my love for you, you never
have to wonder.

It's a perfectly blue,
cloudless day?
That's more
than okay!

Look for me in the wind that blows your hair.
See me in the beautiful sunsets, the
ones that make you stare.

20

Feel me in the warm
summer breeze.
Hug me back when I
give you a big squeeze.

21

When the grass tickles your feet, think of me, and remember how lucky we were that we got to meet.

Picture us together on a
big blue trampoline.
Up and down we go, talking about
our lives, and everything in between.

Most of all, remember that we were
meant for each other's lives.
And when we meet again one day, we'll greet
each other with the biggest hugs and high fives.

Now let's go *chase* the clouds together,
for you and me, we were meant
to be together forever.

Printed in the United States
by Baker & Taylor Publisher Services